Really Brave Tim

1 3 5 7 9 10 8 6 4 2

Copyright © text and illustrations John Prater 1999

John Prater has asserted his right under the
Copyright, Designs and Patents Act, 1988,
to be identified as the author and illustrator of this work

First published in the United Kingdom 1999
by The Bodley Head Children's Books
Random House, 20 Vauxhall Bridge Road, London SW1V 2SA

Random House Australia (Pty) Limited
20 Alfred Street, Milsons Point, Sydney
New South Wales 2061, Australia

Random House New Zealand Limited
18 Poland Road, Glenfield
Auckland 10, New Zealand

Random House South Africa (Pty) Limited
Endulini, 5A Jubilee Road,
Parktown 2193, South Africa

Random House UK Limited Reg. No. 954009

A CIP catalogue record for this book
is available from the British Library

ISBN 0 370 32389 0

Printed in Hong Kong

Really Brave Tim

JOHN PRATER

THE BODLEY HEAD
LONDON

Inside Tim's den sat Billy, Millie, Suki and Tim.
They were boasting.
'I'm not scared of the dark,' said Billy.

Tim kept very quiet. He *was* scared of the dark,
but he didn't want to tell.

And so Billy began:
'There was a noise
from the night, so
I crept outside...

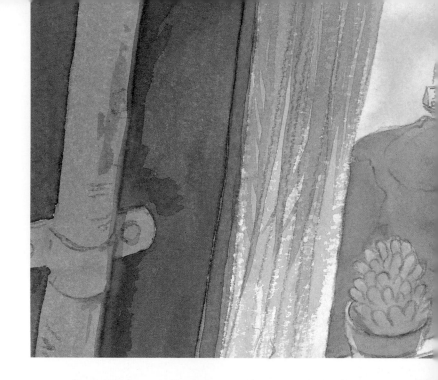

'...through the deep dark forest
to the tangled-up trees...

'...where the goblins were playing football.
But I wasn't scared. I yelled at them – "That's *my* ball. Give it back NOW." And they did. So I went back to sleep.'

'Wow! You *were* brave!' said Millie, Suki and Tim.

Then it was Millie's turn.
'Well, I'm not scared of the
sea,' she said.
Tim kept very quiet. Tim
was scared of the sea, but
he didn't want to tell.

And so Millie began:
'I was swimming deep down
when I dived through the
dark…

'...then I saw a great shark
with terrible teeth.
I climbed on his back and
went for a ride...

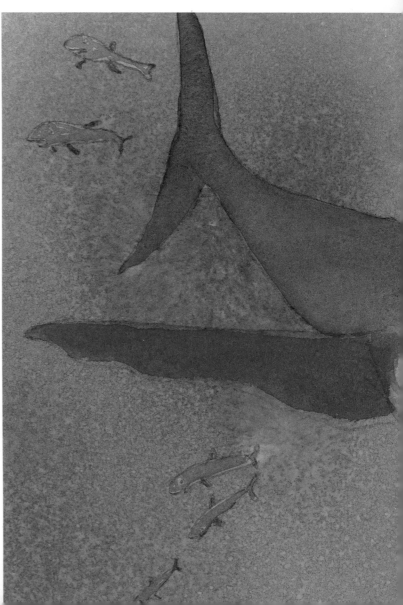

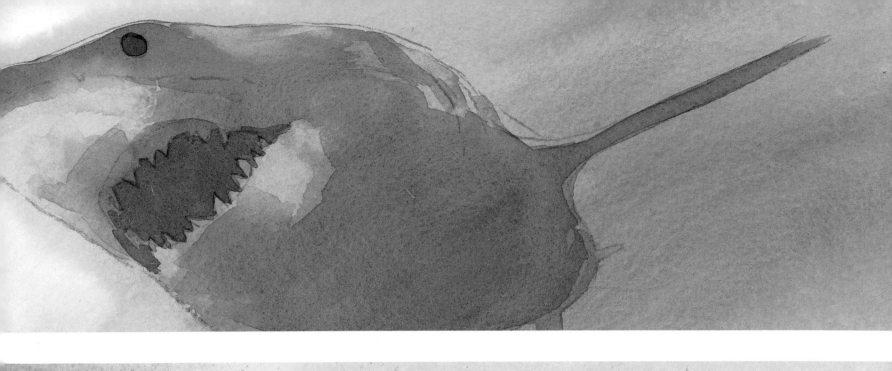

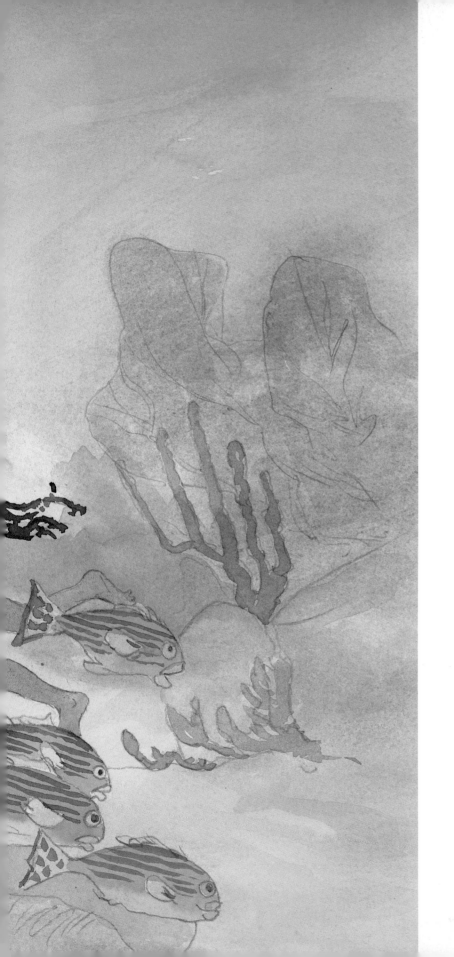

'...and right down at the bottom, on the floor of the ocean I found my lost shoes, which had been washed out to sea. And the shark carried me back to the beach.'

'Wow! You were *really* brave!' said Billy, Suki and Tim.

Then it was Suki's turn.
'Well I'm not scared of heights,'
she said.
Tim kept very quiet. Tim *was*
scared of heights, but he didn't
want to tell.

And so Suki began:
'I had been to the sweetshop,
when a crafty dragon swooped
down and pinched my
peppermints...

'...so I followed him higher and higher to the top of the world...

'...where the dragon was finding my peppermints far too hot. He gave them straight back.'

'Wow! You were *really, really* brave!' said Billy, Millie and Tim.

Then everyone looked
at Tim. They were waiting
for his story. But he was scared
of the dark. He couldn't swim.
He felt dizzy with heights.
He wasn't even sure he could
eat a strong mint!

He was very, very quiet. Then he suddenly noticed something, and cupped his hands over Billy's head.

And so Tim began:

'In my hand there is something that wriggles.
It's squirmy and hairy. It's awfully scary. But
it doesn't frighten me, not one little bit.
Look everyone! It's a...'

'It's a spider!' yelled Billy and Millie and Suki.
'AARGH, LET US OUT!'

Billy, Millie and Suki peeped into the den.
'Wow, you're *really, really, really* brave,' they
said to Tim.
And really brave Tim smiled.
He knew it was true.